RAFIKI

Written and illustrated by
Nola Langner

The Viking Press New York

FOR BELINDA

**With special thanks to my mother, ELSIE SPIERO,
for her cheerful assistance with the scissors work**

The African words in this book are taken from the Swahili language,
which is spoken in East Africa.

First Edition
Copyright © Nola Langner, 1977   All rights reserved
First published in 1977 by The Viking Press, 625 Madison Avenue, New York, N.Y. 10022
Published simultaneously in Canada by The Macmillan Company of Canada Limited
Printed in U.S.A.   1 2 3 4 5 81 80 79 78 77
Library of Congress Cataloging in Publication Data. Langner, Nola.   Rafiki.
Summary: A little girl's arrival at the animals' home in the African jungle
inadvertently provides them with the opportunity to clean their very dirty house.
(1. Jungle stories. 2. Animals—Fiction) I. Title.
PZ7.L268Raf   (E)   76-117   ISBN 0-670-58907-1

Once again it was morning in Africa.
The sun was orange.
And Rafiki walked into the jungle.

As always, the animals woke up in their big
  dirty house.
Every morning it was the same.
The ostrich coughed in the dusty air.
The warthog hid behind the torn curtains.
The rhino stamped on the sandy rug.

The stork washed in the messy sink.
The baboon looked for a clean dish.
The crocodile sat near the cold stove,
   thinking about fish.
And the lion, who was King, yawned.

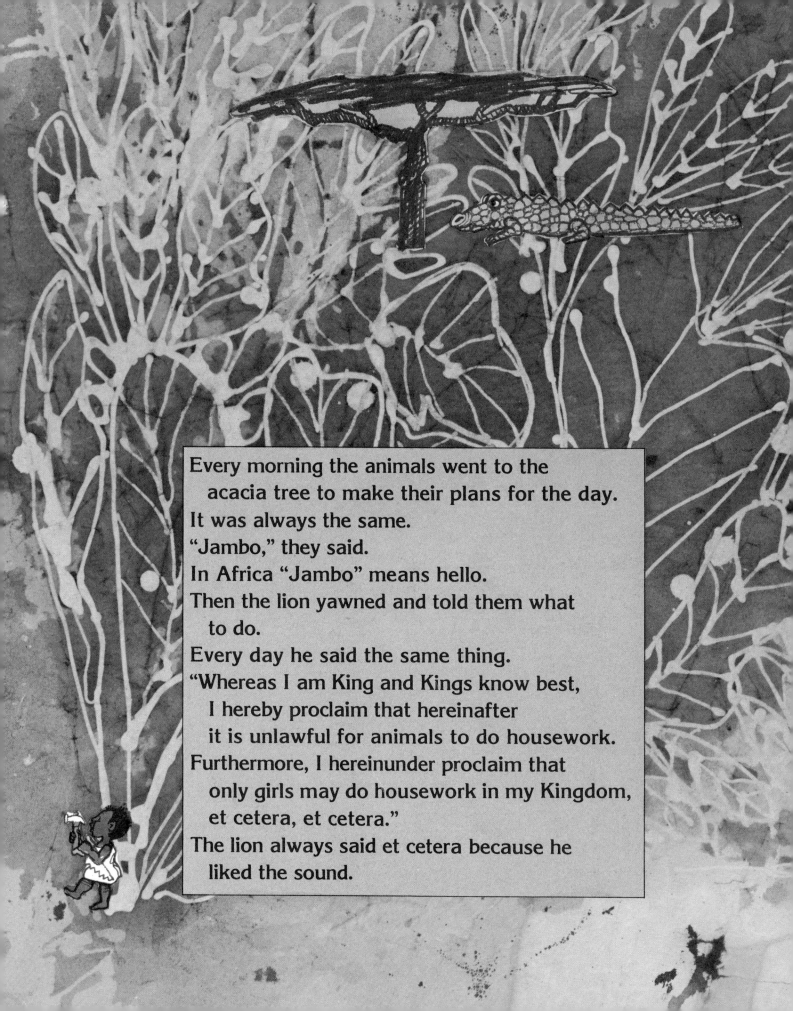

Every morning the animals went to the
   acacia tree to make their plans for the day.
It was always the same.
"Jambo," they said.
In Africa "Jambo" means hello.
Then the lion yawned and told them what
   to do.
Every day he said the same thing.
"Whereas I am King and Kings know best,
   I hereby proclaim that hereinafter
   it is unlawful for animals to do housework.
Furthermore, I hereinunder proclaim that
   only girls may do housework in my Kingdom,
   et cetera, et cetera."
The lion always said et cetera because he
   liked the sound.

After that he always fell asleep.
Some Kings need a lot of rest.
The animals always believed the lion.
They did what he said,
    even though their house got dirtier,
    day after day.
"Kings know best," they said, even though
    their King was usually asleep.
Every day the animals told about the things
    they would do.
It was always the same.

The ostrich spoke first.
"I will go to the plains and run like the wind.
I have such beautiful strong legs."

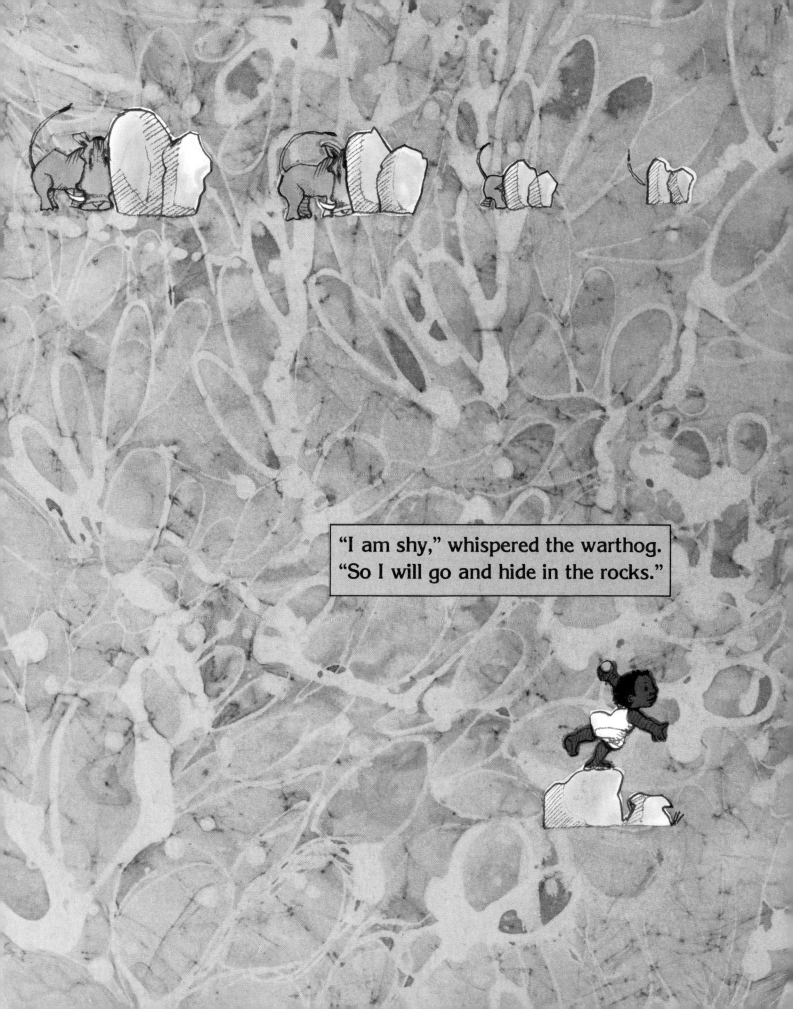

"I am shy," whispered the warthog.
"So I will go and hide in the rocks."

The rhino roared, "I am powerful and large. I think I need to knock down a tree."

Then came the stork.
"I will spread my huge wings and fly up to the clouds.
Maybe today I will see something wonderful down on the ground."
He said that every day.
But he never saw anything.

"I will leap in the trees," yelled the baboon.
"I will make a lot of noise."

The crocodile smiled a big sharp smile.
"I am going to the river to catch a fish."

As always, the lion woke up.
"Today," he said, "I think I will take a nap."
That is what he said every day.

The animals left the acacia tree.
"Kwa heri," they said.
"Kwa heri" means good-bye.
The stork spread his huge wings and flew
    up to the clouds.
He looked for something wonderful down
    on the ground.
Suddenly he stopped flying.
"Amazing!" he said.
Because today he found something.
He flew down closer and there was a little
    girl.
It was Rafiki.
The stork smiled at her.
"Jambo, little girl," he said. "Are you lost?"
"I should say not," said the little girl.
"I'm looking for a good place to build my
    house."

The stork called the animals together.
They took the little girl home.
"Jambo, little girl," they said. "Are you lost?"
"Of course not," said the little girl.
"I'm looking for a good place to build my
  house."

The animals laughed for a long time.
"Little girls don't build houses," they said.

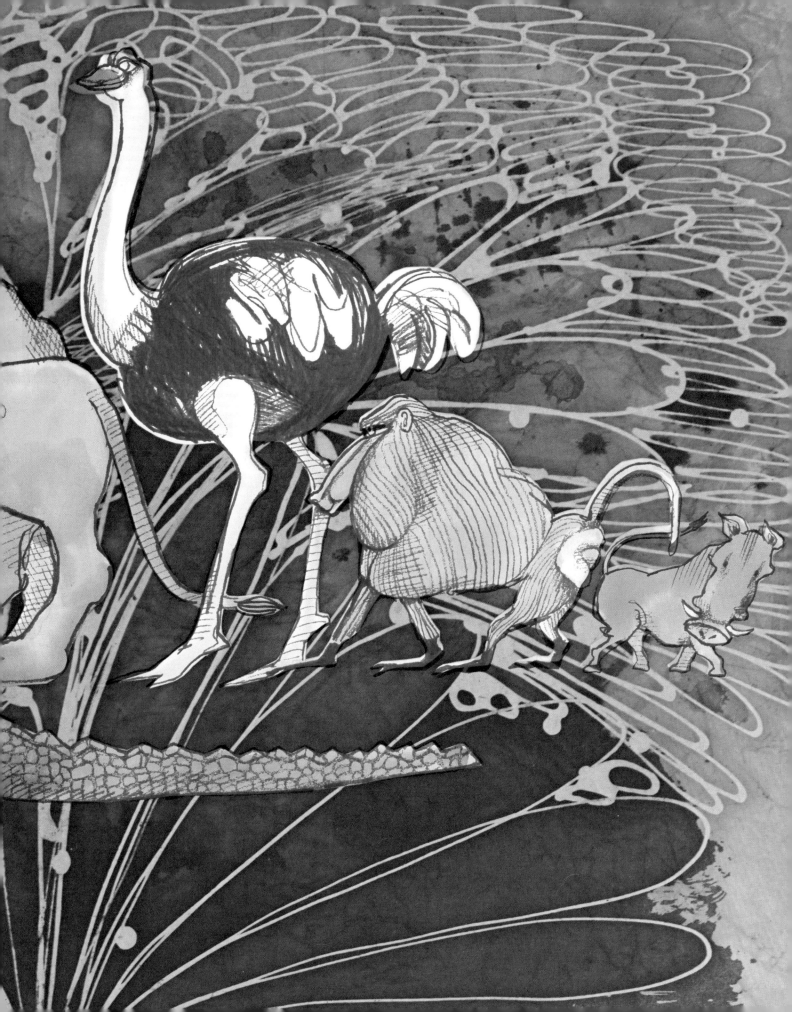

"Oh," said Rafiki, "what do little girls do?"
"They dust," said the ostrich, "like this."
He stretched his beautiful strong legs and
   dusted the house.
"They also sew," said the warthog. "Like this."
He hid behind a curtain and mended all the
   holes.
"What little girls really do best is sweep,"
   said the rhino.
He snorted all the sand into one pile.

"And don't forget cleaning sinks," said the
  stork as he wiped. "Little girls love that."
"Little girls," said the baboon as he scrubbed,
  "always wash dishes."
"And they all know how to cook," said the
  crocodile.
He lit the stove and cooked some fish.

The house was clean and the animals were
    tired.
The animals looked at the little girl to see
    which job she would do first.
Rafiki smiled.
But she didn't speak.
"Please, little girl," begged the baboon,
    "if you work for us you can come to all our
    birthday parties."
"Please, little girl," cried the crocodile,
    "clean our house and we'll be your best
    friends."
Now it was Rafiki's turn to laugh.
She laughed for a long time.
"You just did all the work by yourselves,"
    she said.
The animals were so surprised!
"Oh, my goodness," said the stork.
"What will the lion say?"

They looked at the lion.
Luckily, he was still asleep.

"Let's tell him we did it!" yelled the rhino.
"Maybe we should tell him in the morning," whispered the warthog.
"Maybe Kings don't know best," said the stork.
He spoke very quietly.
By now it was night.
It was time for the animals to go to bed.
"Kwa heri, little girl," they said.
"Kwa heri" also means good night.
"Kwa heri, everyone," said Rafiki.

All that night, while the animals slept,
   Rafiki was busy.
Very busy.

When it was morning, the animals woke up
   as usual.
The sun was orange as usual.
Rafiki was still there.
But somehow everything was different.
There was no dust. The ostrich didn't cough.
No more holes. The warthog could hide.

There was no sand when the rhino stamped on the rug.
The stork had a clean sink.
The baboon found a dish for breakfast.
The crocodile cooked some more fish.
And the lion, of course, still yawned.

Then he looked around.

"Very nice," he said. "Who cleaned everything up?

Was a little girl here?"

"Well, not exactly," said the stork, looking out the window.

"Well, to tell the truth," snorted the rhino, "it was us!"

The lion opened his mouth wide.

Then he roared.

"I like it, I like it," he shouted.

"But you told us not to," croaked the crocodile.

"Don't believe everything you're told," said the lion.

Some Kings never like to admit that they're wrong.

The animals were happy.
"With my strong legs," said the ostrich,
"I could do this every day."
"We all could," they said. "Every day."
"Let's go tell the little girl," yelled the baboon.
The animals went over to the acacia tree.
But today the acacia tree was different too.
Rafiki's house was under it.
And Rafiki was inside.
"Jambo," said the stork, very amazed.
"I guess little girls do build houses after all."
"Jambo," said Rafiki, "they certainly do."
"Zuri sana," said all the animals.
"They certainly do."
In Africa "zuri sana" means wonderful.

The stork put one large wing around Rafiki.
"By the way, little girl," he said,
    "what is your name?"
"My name," she said, "is Rafiki."
"Zuri sana," the animals said.
Because in Africa "Rafiki" means friend.